Inside a House That Is Haunted

A Rebus Read-Along Story

by Alyssa Satin Capucilli
Illustrated by Tedd Arnold

Cartwheel
·B·O·O·K·S·®

SCHOLASTIC INC.
New York Toronto London Auckland Sydney

Library of Congress Cataloging-in-Publication Data

Capucilli, Alyssa.
Inside a house that is haunted: a rebus read-along story / by Alyssa Capucilli;
illustrated by Tedd Arnold.
p. cm.
Summary: A cumulative rhyme in which the spider, ghost, cat, and other
inhabitants of a haunted house wake up and startle each other.
ISBN 0-590-99716-5
1. Rebuses. [1. Haunted houses—Fiction. 2. Stories in rhyme. 3. Rebuses.]
I. Arnold, Tedd, ill. II. Title.
PZ8.3.C1935Il 1998
[E]—dc21 97-38398 CIP AC

12 11 10 9 8 7 6 5 4 3 2   8 9/9 0/0 01 02 03

Printed in Mexico
First Scholastic printing, September 1998

49

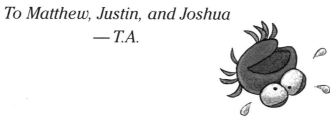

Here is a house that is haunted.

Here is the hand that knocked
on the door
outside a house that is haunted.

Here is the that knocked
on the door

and startled the spider that
dropped to the floor
inside a house that is haunted.

Here is the  that knocked
on the door
and startled the that
dropped to the floor

that frightened the ghost who
awoke and cried, "BOO!"
inside a house that is haunted.

Here is the  that knocked
on the door
and startled the ![spider] that
dropped to the floor
that frightened the ![ghost] who
awoke and cried, "BOO!"

surprising the cat that
jumped and screeched, "MEW!"
inside a house that is haunted.

Here is the 🐾 that knocked
on the door
and startled the 🕷 that
dropped to the floor
that frightened the 👻 who
awoke and cried, "BOO!"
surprising the 🐱 that
jumped and screeched, "MEW!"

that shook up the bats that
swooped through the air
inside a house that is haunted.

Here is the  that knocked
on the door
and startled the that
dropped to the floor
that frightened the who
awoke and cried, "BOO!"
surprising the that
jumped and screeched, "MEW!"
that shook up the that
swooped through the air

and jolted the owl that called,
"Who-Who's there?"
inside a house that is haunted.

Here is the  that knocked
on the door
and startled the  that
dropped to the floor
that frightened the  who
awoke and cried, "BOO!"
surprising the  that
jumped and screeched, "MEW!"
that shook up the  that
swooped through the air
and jolted the  that
called, "Who-Who's there?"

that spooked the mummy who
ran with a shriek
inside a house that is haunted.

Here is the 🖐 that knocked
on the door
and startled the 🕷 that
dropped to the floor
that frightened the 👻 who
awoke and cried, "BOO!"
surprising the 🐱 that
jumped and screeched, "MEW!"
that shook up the 🦇 that
swooped through the air
and jolted the 🦉 that
called, "Who-Who's there?"
that spooked the 🧟 who
ran with a shriek

rattling the skeleton who
moved with a creak
inside a house that is haunted.

Here is the ![hand] that knocked
on the door
and startled the ![spider] that
dropped to the floor
that frightened the ![ghost] who
awoke and cried, "BOO!"
surprising the ![cat] that
jumped and screeched, "MEW!"
that shook up the ![bat] that
swooped through the air
and jolted the ![owl] that
called, "Who-Who's there?"
that spooked the ![mummy] who
ran with a shriek
rattling the ![skeleton] who
moved with a creak

threw open the door,
and heard, "TRICK OR TREAT!"

inside a house that is haunted.